THE TIME WARP TRIO

Your Mother Was a Neanderthal

by Jon Scieszka

illustrated by Lane Smith

A TRUMPET CLUB SPECIAL EDITION

For Jack Dexter,
mathematical magician and
headmaster extraordinaire

Published by The Trumpet Club, Inc.,
a subsidiary of Bantam Doubleday Dell Publishing Group, Inc.,
1540 Broadway, New York, New York 10036.
"A Trumpet Club Special Edition" with the portrayal of a
trumpet and two circles is a registered trademark of
Bantam Doubleday Dell Publishing Group, Inc.

ISBN 0-440-83147-4

This edition published by arrangement with Viking Penguin,
a division of Penguin Books USA Inc.

Printed in the United States of America
January 1995
1 3 5 7 9 10 8 6 4 2
OPM

Cover title hand-lettered by Michele Laporte
Text set in Sabon

ONE

It was like nothing on earth we had ever seen before. Fred, Sam, and I stood in front of a forest of strange trees and giant ferns. A rocky cliff rose behind us. A volcano smoked ahead of us.

But we didn't really notice any of that at first. The first thing we noticed was that the three of us were standing around completely, unbelievably, and absolutely naked.

"We lost everything," yelled Fred. He dove behind the nearest giant fern.

"I don't understand it," said Sam. "This never happens in those other time travel books."

"So why does it have to happen to us?" asked Fred. "This is totally embarrassing."

"We didn't lose everything," I said. "Sam still has his glasses. You've got your hat. And I've got my straw."

"That's all you have? A straw?" asked Fred. "Don't tell me you lost *The Book*."

"Okay, I won't tell you," I said.

"You don't have *The Book*? Oh, man," said Fred. "This time we are *really* cooked. I knew it wouldn't work. There is no way we are going to find *The Book* here in the Stone Age. We'll be lucky if we find anybody who can even talk."

Sam looked around. "So, okay. Things don't look so good."

"Don't look so good?" said Fred. "We have to wait a million years for people to invent talking, writing, and then bookmaking. And all you can say is things don't look so good?"

"According to my calculations," said Sam, "we've probably landed in the year 40,000 B.C. We are completely naked. We have no tools, weapons, or supplies. But we still have one thing."

"Goosebumps?" said Fred.

"No, you jerk. Knowledge. Brainpower. All the learning of modern man," said Sam. He pointed dramatically toward the smoking volcano. "Out there in the prehistoric world, we can still be kings, or at least very popular guys."

Fred and I looked out over the grassy plain.

"Right now I'd settle for some underwear and a slice of pizza," said Fred. Sam pretended he didn't hear that last crack. "With our superior brainpower, we can recreate modern civilization. Observe." He pulled a giant leaf from a bush. "Pants." He held up a piece of vine. "Belt." He tied the leaf on. "Clothes."

Fred and I did the same. We looked pretty ridiculous. But it was a start on civilization.

Fred hopped around in his new leaf shorts.

"*Ug, ug.* Now we learn Reading and Writing. Skip Arithmetic."

A strangled screech echoed in the forest.

I checked the landscape nervously.

"What about Running and Hiding? It sure would spoil my day to get eaten by a dinosaur."

"No, no, no," said Sam. "Brainpower. Dinosaurs and cavemen never lived at the same time." Sam adjusted his leaf. "If this is 40,000 B.C., dinosaurs have been extinct for 65 million years. Cro-Magnon man, our direct ancestor, should just be replacing Neanderthal man."

Sam paused. And at that very second we heard a terrified human scream.

"*Aha!* Man," said Sam.

But then we heard another sound. It was a roar. A very large roar. The kind that comes from a very large, angry, and hungry animal.

"I think it's time for a disappearing act," I said.

"You can do that without *The Book*?" asked Sam.

"Sure," I said, diving behind the nearest fern.

Fred and Sam followed just as a bunch of wild-looking men crashed out of the bushes. They wore raggy skins, had long scraggly hair and beards, and were running as fast as they could.

"Cavemen," whispered Fred.

The tops of the bushes
shook, and the animal
that was chasing them
stuck out its head.

"Dinosaur,"
whispered
Fred.

"Impossible,"
said Sam.
"Dinosaurs are extinct."

The big scaly head turned its beady eyes toward us and roared.

We backed against the rock wall.

"Why don't you go explain that to him," I said. "Then maybe he'll go away."

The dinosaur looked at us and roared again.

We went to the Stone Age to become kings, and were about to become lunch.

5

TWO

But I'm getting way ahead of myself (or really about 42,000 years behind). Let me explain.

My best friends Sam and Fred were hanging around at my house after school as usual. We were trying to finish some annoying math homework—very unusual. If it hadn't been pouring rain, we'd have been long gone.

"I've got a great idea," said Sam.

"I don't need any great ideas," said Fred. "I need the answer to problem 14: 'If Mr. Sleeby walks at an average speed of 2.5 miles per hour, how many miles does he walk in 4 hours?' "

"2.5 miles per hour times 4 hours equals 10 miles," said Sam. "You see, our problem is we've been going about this time-travel business all wrong. We haven't been using our brains."

I looked up. "What do you mean?"

"Well, I've been doing a little research, reading time-travel books—*Half Magic,* Narnia stuff, *A Wrinkle in Time,* and *The Time Machine.*"

"Hey, I saw that movie," said Fred.

"And do you know what people in those books always forget?"

"Food," said Fred. "They never eat in those books."

"No, you Neanderthal," said Sam. "They never pack anything useful to take with them. Like King Arthur would have been amazed by this calculator. The Cheyenne would have been wowed by a Walkman."

"And Blackbeard would have loved an F-16," said Fred.

Sam frowned. "I'm serious. If we just take the right ordinary stuff, people will be convinced we're magic."

I put down my pencil. "But I just learned this great trick," I said. "Watch me roll this straw across my desk using only the invisible powers in one finger. I won't touch it. Watch. Hocus, pocus, straw move-ocus." The straw rolled across my desk with my finger just behind it.

"That's very magical," said Fred. "Especially the way you blow the straw so it rolls."

"You weren't supposed to see that," I said. "I told you to watch my finger."

"But one detail I haven't exactly figured out," continued Sam, "is how to take *The Book* with us so we can get home whenever we want to."

"You call that a detail?" said Fred.

"But I think the trick might be to just hang on to *The Book* right when that green time-traveling mist starts to swirl around."

"It sounds almost too simple to be true," I said.

"Sometimes the best ideas are the simplest," said Sam. "The ancient Greek mathematician Archimedes discovered he could move the world with just a fulcrum, a long enough lever, and a place to stand."

"Archy Meadies?" said Fred. "Wasn't he a shortstop for the Cubs?"

Sam frowned.

Fred slapped him with his hat. "Just kidding, Mr. Brainpower. But what the heck is a fulcrum?"

Sam flipped over his math homework and drew on the back. "The fulcrum is the piece the lever rests on. You put the lever under a big object and over the fulcrum like this . . ."

Fulcrum
(pink pearl eraser)

". . . Pull down the lever. Big object pops up."

"Fascinating," said Fred with a yawn. "But let's get back to time traveling. Where do we go next? Ancient Egypt? Outer space? The future?"

"Well, obviously," said Sam, adjusting his glasses, "the farther back in time we go, the more impressive our things will be."

"Oh, obviously," said Fred.

"So if we go back to prehistoric times, we will be most impressive."

"Oh, most impressive," said Fred.

"Actually, for once, you make great sense," I said to Sam. "I guess we were pretty stupid not to figure it out sooner."

"Speak for yourself," said Sam.

"Well, what are we waiting for?" said Fred. "Let's pack up and head for the Stone Age."

"So what should we take?" I asked.

"Weapons," said Fred.

"Tools," said Sam.

"What about magic tricks?" I asked.

"Weapons," said Fred a little louder.

"Tools," said Sam a little louder.

"Hold it, you guys," I said. "Let's split up. Everybody take whatever you think is best from the house. We'll meet back here in half an hour."

"What about your mom?" said Fred. "I'm still in trouble for breaking your lamp."

"Don't worry," I said. "She won't be home until five. It's only four. We'll take off for the Stone Age at four-thirty and be back at—"

"Four-thirty," said Sam. "With plenty of time to finish homework for Mr. Dexter, and put everything back for your mom."

We scattered. And 30 minutes later, we were standing in my room, loaded for time travel.

Fred held a slingshot and a barbecue fork. A Swiss army knife, a water pistol, and a Walkman hung from his belt. His pockets were stuffed with tapes, marbles, and stick matches.

Sam looked like a walking gadget store. Pens, can openers, potato peelers, scissors, thermometers, buckles, zippers, paper clips, safety pins, hammers, pliers, and a folding saw hung from every available belt loop and pocket.

I wore my magician's top hat and filled my pockets with magic rings, my wand, flash paper, coins, scarves, ropes, and juggling balls. I held *The Book* with both hands.

I looked in the index
for "Cavemen,"
but found only
"Cave painting—
p. 123."

"Time Warp Trio,
prepare to meet
your ancestors," I
said and flipped
The Book open to
page 123.
There was a
picture of a cave
painting with a
spiral of stars,
moons, handprints,
and three stick figures. And right on cue, the
green time-traveling mist swirled around our feet.

"Hang on to that book," said Sam.

"Sam, I have to hand it to you," said Fred.
"Most of the time you are an obnoxious know-
it-all." The mist rose to our necks. "But for once
in your life, you've come up with a great idea."

The mist closed over our heads and we were
gone to the time before time.

THREE

The dinosaur roared and shook the branches.

"Yeah, Mr. Great Idea. Go tell him he's extinct," said Fred.

We flattened ourselves against the rock. We were trapped.

"Forget talking," whispered Sam. "Joe, how about some magic? Quick."

I held up my straw.

"I don't think so," said Fred. "Grab these rocks. Maybe we can scare it off."

Fred picked up a stone and leaned back to throw. That's when his leaf started to slip. The dinosaur roared. Fred tried to pull up his leaf pants with one hand, and throw with the other. He hopped on one leg and then crashed into Sam and me and knocked us all into a heap. The dinosaur roared again and then suddenly hic-cupped and laughed.

Sam and I looked at each other.

The dinosaur laughed.

We all looked closer.

The dinosaur laughed and shook and then lost its head. I mean it really lost its head. The head fell out of the bushes and rolled down a little hill. The bushes kept laughing.

The bushes shook again and three girls stum-bled out, laughing so hard they could hardly stand up. They were about the same size as us and wore animal-skin dresses. The tallest had long, wavy red hair. One had short blonde hair and a necklace of shells. And the third girl cov-ered her eyes and wouldn't look right at us.

We stared at the dinosaur head, then the girls. The shy one hiccupped and they all cracked up again, laughing and pointing at us and then the head.

"It wasn't that funny," said Fred, fixing his leaf.

The cavegirl with the necklace seemed to be the leader. She calmed her friends down and mo-tioned for us to come closer. She sized us up as

we approached. The red-haired girl signaled
something with her hands. Her friends looked at
us and cracked up again.

"Knock it off," yelled Fred. "Or I'll brain you
with this rock like I was planning to."

All three girls opened their eyes in surprise.
They made signs with their hands in front of their
mouths.

Sam imitated the sign and nodded. "Yes, we talk." He pointed to them. "You talk?"

They looked puzzled.

"Do you have any form of verbal communication?" asked Sam. He waved his hands in circles under his chin.

The tall red-haired girl nodded. She ran to the bushes and came back with a cone-shaped thing made of sticks and covered with skin. She lifted the small end to her lips and roared a very loud and very convincing dinosaur roar.

We all jumped. The girls fell on each other laughing again.

"Very funny," said Fred. "We go back to the Stone Age to be kings, and we wind up doing Stupid Human Tricks for cavegirls."

We took a closer look at the dinosaur head. It was made out of the same sticks and skin as the megaphone. The eyes were clear red stones. The teeth were made of sharpened bones.

"Let me try to talk to them," I said. I put one hand on my chest. "Joe." I touched Sam. "Sam." Then Fred. "Fred." I repeated, "Joe. Sam. Fred."

The leader nodded and pointed to us. "Joe. Sam. Fred." Then she pointed to herself. "Nat-

Li." She held her red-haired friend by the arm. "Lin-Say." Then she pointed to her hiccupping pal. "Jos-Feen."

I repeated, "Nat-Li. Lin-Say. Jos-Feen."

Nat-Li clapped and smiled. Jos-Feen hiccupped again and looked away.

"Hey, I think we're talking," said Sam.

"Isn't that special," said Fred. "Now let's invent the alphabet, write *The Book*, and get out of here."

The girls talked and signed to each other. Then Nat-Li spoke to us. "Joe, Sam, Fred." She pointed to the volcano in the distance. "Ma."

"I think they want us to follow them," I said.

"But what if they're cannibals and are taking us home to their mom so she can cook us up for dinner?" said Fred.

"Not very likely," said Sam. "Most human cultures had very strict taboos against eating their own kind."

Something howled in the fern forest behind us.

"We're not going to find *The Book* lying around here," I said. "And if we do stay here, we might just end up being someone else's dinner."

"That could be a problem," said Fred. "Let's go see Ma."

Lin-Say picked up her megaphone. Nat-Li and Jos-Feen lifted the fake dinosaur head. And we followed them toward the smoking volcano.

"I wonder why they were scaring those other caveguys away," said Sam. I looked at the sharpened bones on the dinosaur head bobbing up and down ahead of us. I didn't want to say anything, but I had an uneasy feeling we were about to find out why.

FOUR

We followed the three girls up a winding path through the jungle. They walked quickly and silently. We had to run, hop, and jump to keep up with them.

"*Ouch . . . oooch . . . ahhh . . . eee . . .*" Sam yelped with every step. "My feet are killing me."

"Invent shoes," said Fred.

"And I hope they work better than these pants," I said.

Weird jungle noises surrounded us. Thorny branches scratched us. Sharp stones poked our feet. In five minutes we were bleeding, sore-footed, and exhausted.

The girls hiked along like they were strolling down a sidewalk.

"Are we there yet?" moaned Sam.

"I'm hungry," said Fred.

"I'm thirsty," I said.

And suddenly we were there—standing at the edge of a clearing, staring at an opening in the white rock cliff.

"A real cave," I said.

"Real cavemen," said Sam. "Who will gladly make us their leaders, once we bring them civilization."

Nat-Li motioned for us to sit down outside. Sam and I sat. Lin-Say pushed Fred's head and motioned for him to sit too.

"Okay, okay. Don't get so pushy," said Fred.

Lin-Say made a face and imitated Fred. "O-kay o-kay."

Jos-Feen laughed. Nat-Li ran into the cave.

We looked around the clearing and listened to the sound of voices in the cave. A blue-gray line of smoke from the volcano above us drifted across the bottom edge of the sun. A very large bird flew in circles high above us.

Fred looked around. "I don't know, you guys. This looks a bit strange. Where is everybody? What's taking so long? They're probably trying to decide whether to roast us or boil us. I wish I still had my Swiss army knife."

"You are so paranoid," said Sam. "I'm sure Nat-Li went to tell the leader of her clan that she found three magical guys. He's probably just getting dressed up in his best outfit to greet us and make a good impression. Primitive man believed in magic. So try to act magical."

"O-kay o-kay," said Lin-Say.

Nat-Li appeared at the mouth of the cave and called, "Joe Sam Fred."

Standing next to her was a figure dressed, just as Sam had predicted, in what was definitely the clan's best outfit. It was a giant bearskin cape, trimmed with feathers and topped with a bear-mask hood complete with what looked like the original owner's teeth.

"*Aha*—their leader," said Sam. "Let me do the talking."

We stood up and approached the scary-looking bear figure, trying our best to act magical.

"Greetings, oh powerful leader," said Sam, raising one hand, palm out. "We are men of strong magic." Sam flexed both arms. "Who have come to give you much knowledge." Sam pointed to his head. "Fire. The wheel. Music. Cartoons."

The leader didn't move or make a sound.

"Very impressive," whispered Fred.

Sam frowned. "And we, uh . . . of course, brought you a . . . a . . . gift!"

The bear leader stared at us.

Sam snatched Fred's hat off his head and held it out. "Here is the headpiece of our bears—the Cubs. Baby bears, you know. Little guys. Cubs. Gift. Us. You."

"Hey, that was my best hat," said Fred.

The leader took the hat and examined it closely, turning it over and pulling at it. The leader took off the bear-head mask and put on Fred's hat. And we almost dropped dead of surprise. The bearskinned leader was a woman. But that wasn't the surprise. The surprise was that she was a woman we knew.

"Joe," gasped Fred. "It's your mom."

I blinked my eyes. Except for the bearskin outfit and prehistoric surroundings, it definitely looked like my mom.

"Mom?" I said.

The leader looked startled for a second, then placed her hand on her chest and said, "Ma."

"Wow," said Fred. "Listen, I'm sorry about

22

breaking Joe's lamp and everything and if you can get us back home and out of this Stone Age I'll never do anything bad with Joe ever again for the rest of my life I mean it. Do you have *The Book*? Can you do it? Huh? Can you?"

Ma looked over the three of us like she had something in mind for us. Then she said, "Nat-Li," and pointed to the cave.

Nat-Li took Sam's hand and led us into the cool, dark cave. It smelled faintly sweet, like dried flowers and cooking soup. Small fires lit the huge inside and cast strange shadows on the rock walls. We stumbled along in a line behind Nat-Li to the back of the cave. I could just barely see people around the fires as my eyes adjusted to the dim light inside.

"Joe, I will never again say anything bad about your mom as long as I live," said Fred.

We came to a smaller cave off the main cave. Nat-Li motioned for us to go first.

"I can't believe she's here to save us."

"I don't know, Fred," I said. "I don't really think that's my mom. She seems a little . . . different, you know?"

Sam, Fred, and I stepped into the smaller cave.

24

"Oh, she's just doing that because she has to pretend she doesn't know us in front of everybody else."

Then we heard a wooden *clunk* sound behind us.

We turned around and saw Nat-Li, Lin-Say, and Jos-Feen smiling at us from the other side of huge wooden bars that had been roped together.

"We're trapped," yelled Fred. "Let us out, you cannibals!"

"O-kay o-kay," said Lin-Say.

Jos-Feen and Nat-Li looked at us in a hungry sort of way.

"So much for social taboos," said Sam.

Fred and I shook the bars. They didn't budge an inch.

Ma stood with her arms folded across her chest and her new Cubs hat sitting crazily on the top of her wild hair, eyeing us carefully. She looked like she definitely had something in mind for us.

FIVE

We were prisoners in the cave. But something was funny. No one was really treating us like prisoners. We were more like guests of honor.

Nat-Li brought us shirt-and-pants kinds of things made out of skin and fur. Jos-Feen brought us hot vegetable soup in wooden bowls.

"This isn't so bad afer all," said Fred, slurping down the last of his soup. "I guess they don't need much of our help with fire, cooking, clothes, and all of that civilization stuff."

"So why are they keeping us in here and treating us so nicely?" said Sam.

I had an idea why, but it involved human sacrifice and wasn't very appetizing. "Let's think," I said. "A picture of a cave painting got us here, so a cave painting can probably get us home. We're already in a cave. All we have to do is find the painting."

"How about back there?" said Fred, nodding toward the shadows at the back of our cave.

"Prehistoric people believed paintings had magical powers to control things like the animals they hunted," said Sam. "They wouldn't put us in the same place as their most powerful magic. The painting is probably somewhere out there in the big cave."

I looked out through the wooden bars. The main cave was as big as Grand Central Station. And it kind of looked like it too. The side walls curved up into the darkness. It was too dark to see if there were any paintings on the walls.

"If I had my saw we could be out of here in five minutes," said Sam.

"If I had my F-16 we could be out of here in five seconds," said Fred.

I watched groups of people moving from fire to fire. That's when it struck me.

"Hey, you know what's strange?" I said.

"Yeah. Sitting around in a cave dressed like Fred Flintstone is pretty strange," said Fred.

"No. I mean about these people. They're all girls. I haven't seen one guy yet."

Sam looked out the bars next to me. "You're

27

right. No guys. Maybe they're some kind of cave Amazons. But I've never heard of that before."

"You haven't heard of a lot of things before," said Fred. "Like time travelers losing all their clothes. Do Amazons eat people?"

"Not to my recollection," said Sam, adjusting his glasses in that scholarly way of his. "But now I would recommend that we definitely escape as soon as possible because Amazons were not really fond of guys in general."

"That settles it," said Fred. "We're out of here." And he started tugging on the bars.

Sam picked up a stick and started scratching in the sand as he mumbled to himself. "If one of us can saw through half a bar with a sharp stone in 20 minutes, and we need to saw through 4 bars to escape, it should take us . . . 20 minutes times 4 bars times 2 halves . . . 160 minutes of sawing. But if we had 3 sharp stones and all 3 of us sawed at the same time, that would be . . ."

"Maybe I could show them the straw trick and impress them enough so they'll at least let us look around the cave," I said.

"Uh-oh," said Fred. "Forget the math and the magic. It looks like we've got visitors."

The main entrance to the cave was suddenly lit by torches. Ma, Nat-Li, Lin-Say, and Jos-Feen led the pack of cavewomen over to our cage. The flickering torchlight cast evil-looking shadows on everyone's face. Ma smiled and gave us the same look I've seen Fred give a slice of pizza.

Ma motioned. The wooden bars swung up and into the darkness. The cavewomen surrounded us and we followed Ma toward the entrance.

"If you see a cave painting, make a run for it," I called over my shoulder to Fred and Sam.

"*Shhh,*" said Fred. "Don't give away the plan."

Nat-Li, walking next to us, smiled.

"It doesn't matter," said Sam. "They can't understand a word we say. We could tell them we were planning to run away or we could tell them the Pledge of Allegiance. It would all sound the same to them. Okay, Lin-Say?"

Lin-Say nodded and smiled, "O-kay."

Fred started thinking. You can always tell when Fred's thinking because he sticks his tongue out.

"They don't understand what we say . . . but they do understand how we say . . . I've got it."

We approached the entrance and saw the reddish orange light of sunset across the sky. Someone was slowly beating a drum.

"The oldest trick in the book," said Fred smiling.

"Not the old What's-that-on-your-shirt? gag," said Sam.

"No, no," said Fred. "The old What's-that-behind-you? gag."

The drum beat louder and a little faster.

"I don't get it," I said.

"They won't understand *what* we say, but they will understand *how* we say something."

"So?" I said, trying to ignore the drumbeat.

"When I give the signal, we all point to the left, look scared out of our minds, and yell, 'Oh, no! Woolly mammoth!' " said Fred. "They turn to look left. We run right."

Nat-Li, Lin-Say, and Jos-Feen walked next to us, watching Fred closely and listening to every word.

"That is so stupid," said Sam. "It will never work. It's too simple."

"Do you have a better idea, Archimedes?" said Fred.

Ma led the way out of the cave. The sky glowed an amazing orange and purple in the west. A full yellow moon was just beginning to rise in the east. Two women pounded the beat on a huge drum. A crackling fire blazed in the middle of a circle of stones. The flames shot up ten feet high and sent sparks flying up out of sight. The drum beat faster. I looked at Fred. The drum beat faster. Sam looked at Fred. The drum beat faster. Ma raised her hand. The drum stopped.

In the sudden silence, Fred nodded his head.

Fred, Sam, and I pointed to our left and all together yelled, "Oh, no! Woolly mammoth!"

And, believe it or not, everyone looked to the left. We looked at each other for one surprised split second, and then ran for the woods on our right. We crashed blindly through dead sticks and a tangle of vines and bushes. The dim light grew even dimmer under the trees and giant ferns. We heard the cavewomen's surprised yells behind us. The drum started pounding again.

We dodged around black shapes and under hanging things we could only half see, running until the drumbeat began to fade. We turned to avoid something large and dark in front of us and suddenly found ourselves running in midair.

We landed hard.

Everything went black.

SIX

O*hhh*, my aching head," moaned Sam's voice.

"*Aaaahhhh,*" groaned Fred's voice.

"We're alive," I said.

"Are you sure?" said Sam. "My head is pounding. I can't move. I can't breathe. And I can't see a thing."

I tried to move but couldn't. Something was weighing me down.

"You can hear, can't you?" I said.

"Yeah."

"So we're not dead."

"But it sure smells like something died," said Fred.

I gave a sniff. It smelled like two or three things had died . . . and taken their old sneakers off at the same time.

"Maybe we are dead," said Sam. "Maybe this

is what being dead is like—all dark and quiet and smelly."

Fred and I thought about this for a few dark, quiet, and smelly moments. It was not a comforting thought.

"What's that noise?" said Fred.

We strained to hear a faint murmuring sound.

"Sounds like human voices," I said.

We listened again.

"It is human voices," said Sam. He screamed, *"Help! Help! We're not dead. Get us out of here!"*

"Uh, Sam," I said.

"Yes?"

"What if they're not friendly people?"

"Oh, right. I didn't think of that."

"Too late," said Fred's voice. "Here they come, whoever they are."

We held our breath and listened to the noises get louder and closer. Now it didn't sound so much like human voices. Now it sounded more like animal noises.

"Sounds like monkeys," said Sam. "Maybe it's a band of wild apes. Maybe it's a bunch of hungry cave bears. Maybe it's—"

"*Shhhh,*" I whispered. "Maybe they'll go away."

And at that very second, the smelly thing covering us was pulled back. Cool air and faint light washed over us. We found ourselves face to face with a big hairy ape.

"*Ahhhhhhhhhh!*" Sam, Fred, and I all screamed together.

The hairy ape jumped back.

Without the heavy cover on us, we found we could sit up and move again . . . though not too swiftly. I still felt like I just stepped off a bad amusement park ride. Our eyes adjusted to the light. I looked around and figured we must have been knocked out all night. We were sitting in a dirt pit covered with a low roof made from a bunch of logs piled on a fallen tree. There was one hole in the roof where we must have fallen through, and another that looked like a small doorway near the ground.

A whole group of hairy ape-men with ragged animal skins tied on them surrounded us. They looked us over like we were monkeys in the zoo.

"Hey, they're caveguys," said Fred.

"The same guys we saw running from the girls' fake dinosaur," said Sam.

I looked at the scruffy bunch of guys. The biggest one with the beard definitely looked familiar. He approached us cautiously, making noises that sounded like "Hoot, hoot." He held out one gnarly hand, black with dirt.

I took his hand and shook it. "Glad to meet you, Mr. Hoot. My name is Joe. Sorry to drop in on your pit—er, house here."

Dirty bits of hide and fur hung from sticks. Piles of dead leaves covered the dirt floor. And the whole place smelled like a combination of old socks, bad cheese, and public bathrooms. "Reminds me of your room, Fred."

The bearded guy wiggled my hand and hooted again. The rest of his gang shuffled their feet in the dirt and hooted along.

"Hoot, hoot, to you too," I said. "Oh, and these are my friends Fred and Sam."

The big guy pointed to Fred and Sam. "Ug a ug."

"Close enough," I said.

The big guy put his hand on his chest and said, "Duh."

"No kidding," said Sam.

"Duh," the caveguy repeated.

I said, "Duh. Okay, Duh. Too bad about your name, but thanks for letting us use your . . . uh, place." I looked around the pit again. It really was a pit.

"No chance these guys would have *The Book*," said Fred.

"Boog?" said Duh.

"Yeah, a book. You know. A thing about this

big." Fred held out two hands pressed together. "With pages. A magic book."

"Boog. Boog." The leader, Duh motioned to one of the other men. He started digging under a pile of sticks and dirt in the back of the pit.

"I can't believe it," said Sam. "These guys live in a hole in the ground and they have *The Book*? Maybe they aren't as dumb as they look."

The little guy found what he was looking for and brought it to Duh.

"You just never know with magic," I said.

Duh took the animal skin wrap and handed it to me and smiled. "Boog."

Joe, Sam, and I crowded around the package.

"Hello magic book. Good-bye Stone Age," cheered Fred. "I never thought I could be this happy to get back to my math homework."

I unwrapped the skin as fast as I could and held up a completely rotten, maggot-covered . . . piece of meat.

Duh smiled and nodded. "Boog." He took a bite, rubbed his stomach, and handed it to us again. "Boog."

Fred, Sam, and I gagged and started crawling for fresh air through the hole in the low roof.

We hit the space between two logs at the same time and all tried to get out first. The caveguys grabbed us and pulled us back.

Duh pointed outside and shook his head, "Ug Caa." He made a weird face with his teeth showing and his hands in front of him like claws. "Ug Caa."

Fred made a funny gurgling noise. "Let me go or I'm going to Ug Caa all over you."

Fred broke loose from the guy holding him and squeezed between the logs into the fresh air. Sam and I were just about to follow when we heard Fred scream the loudest scream I've ever heard Fred scream.

"Caaa!!!"

SEVEN

Fred dove back inside like a bullet. A split second later something large, furry, and mad crashed into the logs behind him. Dirt and dead leaves showered down on us. A huge paw with wicked long claws shot between the logs and swiped the air. Everyone dove for the ground. Through the cracks and holes between the logs I could see fangs, claws, and a cat as big as a small bus.

The gigantic cat swatted at the roof logs and roared its disappointment at missing a meal. More dirt and dead leaves rained down on us. And then, with one log-creaking bounce, the cat jumped and was gone.

Duh uncovered his head. "Caa."

"Cat?" said Fred. "That was no cat. Why

didn't you tell me there was a monster with fangs out there?"

"Most likely a saber-toothed cave cat," said Sam.

"Thank you once again, Mr. Superior Brain-power. I feel so much better now that I know the name of the thing that almost ate me for breakfast. Now do you have any bright ideas on how to get us out of this jam?"

Sam looked at the raggedy bunch of cavemen crouched in the dirt around us. "Okay, let's look at this logically." He picked up a stick and drew a dot and a letter in the dirt. "We are at point A, a hole in the ground with a bunch of guys with no weapons, no tools, and quite possibly no brains."

The cavemen looked at Sam's drawing and hooted.

"We would like to get to point B." He drew another dot and labeled it B. "Joe's room in New York."

Duh and the rest of the cavemen looked closely at the marks in the dirt.

"But the only way to get to B is go past C, a rather large killer cat, into D, the cave, to find

E, the cave painting." Sam ended with a wild flourish of dots, lines, a triangle-headed cat, an arc for the cave, and three stick figures for the painting.

"Do you follow?"

The caveguys studied Sam's drawings and nodded and grunted to themselves.

"But how do we do that?" asked Fred.

"How do we do that?" said Sam, tapping his head with his stick. "How? *Hmmmm*. Now that's a whole different question. Magic, I guess."

Sam and Fred turned to me.

"I've still got my straw," I said, hopefully.

"Would you forget that stupid straw trick. We need some big magic," said Fred. "Why didn't you learn spells to make us invisible, or gigantic, or able to blast fire out of our eyes, or something useful like that?"

"I didn't think we'd need any magic if we kept *The Book* with us."

We all stared at Sam's drawing again, looking from A to B, worrying about C and D, wondering how we would ever find E.

"Now I really wish we had some weapons,"

said Fred. "One blast of an Uzi would turn that monster into a scaredy-cat."

Sam looked up. "As Archimedes once said— Eureka."

"We're going to make machine guns?" I said.

"No. We're going to scare the cat," said Sam.

"With what? Your good looks?" said Fred.

Sam pretended not to hear. "With the one thing man has power over, that the animal does not." Sam stood up and paused for effect. "Fire."

"Hey, yeah," said Fred. "That always works in those Tarzan movies."

"But where do we get the fire?" I said. "We lost our matches. And I think these guys eat everything raw."

Fred gagged. "Don't mention eating again."

Sam broke his stick and began rubbing the two pieces together. "We'll invent fire." He rubbed and rubbed. The cavemen watched closely. The sticks got warm. I took over and rubbed. The sticks stayed warm. Fred grabbed the sticks and rubbed. The cavemen hooted. Fred rubbed. The cavemen hooted. Fred rubbed harder. The cavemen hooted. Fred rubber harder. And then . . . the sticks broke.

Fred fell over backward. "This is never going to work. Joe, you must remember some magic."

One of the cavemen picked up the sticks and tried rubbing them together.

I thought about magic to scare the cat. I thought about my straw trick and suddenly had an idea. "How about this," I said, pulling out the straw.

Fred rolled over. "If you show that straw one more time I'm going to take it and personally shove it—"

I took a jagged piece of rock from the ground and used it to cut one end of the straw in a V. I put it to my lips and blew a blast on my new straw horn. The caveguys' eyes bugged out.

I wrapped the fur cover around me and danced around, waving my arms and honking the straw. The caveguys dove for the ground again.

"Now that's how you scare a cat," said Sam.

I threw off the fur, and cut the straw into three pieces and made a point at the end of each piece. "That's how *we* scare a cat," I said, handing Fred and Sam a straw.

"What do you mean we?" asked Sam.

"I mean three heads and three straws are better than one."

Fred grabbed the fur and wrapped it around the three of us.

"Do we really want to do this?" said Sam. "Maybe we should think this through."

Fred stuck two branching sticks behind our heads and said, "Horns."

The cavemen stayed frozen on the ground, looking at us in bug-eyed amazement. Duh stared at us and touched the fur with one careful finger. Fred blew a blast on his straw. Duh jumped five feet.

"Okay, you guys," said Fred. "This is it. We have to charge out there and look like the meanest two-horned, three-headed beast on earth."

We shuffled up to the opening at one end of the pit where the roof met the ground. "And blow your horn like your life depends on it," I said.

"I think it does," said Sam.

Duh pointed outside. "Caa?"

"You said it," said Fred. "Ready, set, *go!*"

And the meanest two-horned, three-headed, straw-honking beast on the planet charged outside to face down one saber-toothed prehistoric cat.

EIGHT

One of our horns stuck between two logs and stayed there. Sam tripped and fell between Fred and me. We didn't really charge outside. We more or less fell outside.

Then I saw it.

Caa, the cat, was crouched next to a tree not thirty feet away. Fred was right. This was no cat. This was five hundred pounds of muscle, big claws, and long, sharp saber teeth. And it was staring at us like we were its next breakfast snack.

I turned into a statue. I couldn't get my muscles to move. My throat dried up and refused to push any air to my straw.

Sam crawled around under the fur honking, yelling, and trying to find a spot to poke his head out.

The giant cat laid his ears back just like I've seen
my cat do before he pounces. Fred blew his straw
and waved one fur covered arm. The cat lowered
into a crouch. I squeaked and waved one arm.
The cat was just about to jump, when Sam found
an opening and poked his head out next to our
feet. He blew one piercing straw honk.

The surprised cat jumped straight up and kind
of half flipped backward in midair. A two-
headed beast was one thing. But a two-headed
beast suddenly growing another head was something not to be messed with.

The cat gave us one last look, then took off into the woods.

We threw off the smelly fur and jumped around tooting our straws and slapping high fives. Duh and his caveguys peeked out of the pit.

"Come on out and breathe the fresh air, Duh," said Fred. "The three-headed, one-horned honker beast has won!"

"Caa?" asked Duh.

"Caa *voom*," said Fred.

It felt so good to be alive and out of the smelly pit. We all laughed and hopped around like crazy men.

Duh slowly crawled out, checking all around him. The rest of the men followed him. They all stood blinking in the sunlight, not quite sure what to do.

"So much for point C," said Sam. "But perhaps we should consider a way to reach our ultimate goal, point B, without returning to point D for E."

Duh, the cavemen, and Fred looked at Sam like he was crazy.

I translated. "He's glad we got rid of the cat,

but he doesn't want to go back to the cave to look for the cave painting."

"Come on, you chicken," said Fred. "If we all march to the cave we can take on Ma."

The caveguys suddenly got very wide-eyed and quiet.

"You guys look like you saw a ghost," said Fred. "All I said was *Ma*."

Three guys dove back under the log pile.

"Ug Ma," said Duh. "Ug Ma." He held his hands up like claws and showed his teeth.

"Ah, that's just a bearskin and a head. Just like the dinosaur head," said Fred. "I'm not afraid of those fakes."

Duh shook his head. "Ma."

"I don't know," said Sam. "Maybe Duh knows something we don't know."

"They probably have the cave painting, and they definitely have my hat," said Fred. "So let's go."

"Let's not and say we did," said Sam. "Maybe we can make our own *Book*."

I looked at the scrawny bunch of caveguys blinking in the sunlight. "These guys are our ancestors. And they don't know anything about fire, clothing, or shelter. The women have figured out all that stuff. Even if we don't find a cave painting or *The Book,* we should at least get the men and women together. Otherwise we might not have a human future to go back to."

"Excellent point," said Sam. "In the interest of survival of the species, I guess we should get these guys out of their pit and help them meet a few girls. But how are we ever going to get these prehistoric nerds to help? They'll run away if you even say 'Boo.' "

"You're right," said Fred. "But what if we said something else?' Fred jumped up on a stump. "Okay, caveguys, listen up. We are going to the cave. You are coming to help us."

"Very convincing," said Sam. "They look *real* interested."

"But what's in it for you?" said Fred. "Boog."
The men looked up.

"Lots of *boog.* Bit heaping piles of *boog.* Squirming, stinking mountains of *boog.* All the *boog* you can eat." Fred pointed toward the volcano. "Onward to *boog,* men!"

The men milled around. They looked at Fred. They looked at their leader, Duh. You could

51

almost see Duh thinking. He furrowed his brow, and then finally walked toward Fred.

Fred chanted, "Boog, boog, it's good for your heart. The more you eat, the more you—"

The caveguys joined in. "Boog, boog . . ."

Sam and I honked our straws. Everyone followed Fred and Duh down the path toward the cave. We were on our way to boog, *The Book*, and Home Sweet Civilization Home.

And we probably would have made it. But something rumbled.

"What was that?" I said.

The something rumbled again. The ground shook beneath our feet. It wobbled and jumped and shook like jello, throwing everyone down.

"Earthquake!" yelled Sam.

And it was.

NINE

Trees shook.

Rocks crashed.

The ground wiggled and suddenly split open right behind us.

The cavemen's logpile home fell into the cracked earth and disappeared. Then everything stopped. No birds, no bugs, no prehistoric beasts made a sound.

I sat up and dusted off my animal skin. "That could have been ... I mean, that was almost ... we were almost ..."

"Smashed into little bits and buried under a ton of prehistoric garbage!" screamed Sam.

"Calm down, Sam," said Fred. "Things could be worse."

"Oh yeah? How?" said Sam, looking a little wild-eyed and crazy. "We're trapped 40,000 years in the past. Everything we meet tries to eat us. And now even the ground underneath us is falling apart. And you say things could be worse? How could things be worse?" Sam smacked himself on the forehead with the palm of his hand.

Duh and his men stood up carefully and moved to the edge of the new ravine. They looked down at the pile of broken logs at the bottom. They looked at Sam. Duh let out a wild yell, then smacked himself in the head. And all at once, all of the guys started yelling, moaning, and smacking their heads.

"That's how," said Fred.

Sam yelled. The caveguys yelled. Sam moaned. The caveguys moaned.

"And how," I said.

The noise of Sam, Duh, and the caveguys grew louder and louder, and suddenly *much* louder.

Duh stopped beating himself up, listened, and then yelled something that sounded like "Woo Maa! Woo Maa!" Everyone ran for the trees and left Fred, Sam, and me staring at each other.

"Woo Maa?" said Fred. "What's Woo Maa?"

Sam stood frozen, looking off into the space over our heads.

"I don't know," I said. "But I think we've lost Sam."

Sam croaked, "Woo . . . woo . . . woo . . . ma . . . ma . . . ma—"

"We've definitely lost him," said Fred.

Sam raised his arm to point and croaked again, "Oh, no. Woolly mammoth!"

"He's snapped. He thinks we're the cave-women," I said. "It's okay, Sam. It's me, Joe."

And right then I was stopped by an ear-popping trumpeted blast of noise. Fred and I turned to look behind us. There, standing at the edge of the clearing, not twenty feet away from us, stood the largest and most crazed-looking beast you will never want to see as long as you live. You've seen them in books. And you've seen their relatives in zoos. And I'm telling you, you don't need to see them any closer.

"Oh, no," I said.

"*Woolly mammoth!*" yelled Fred.

At that moment I understood where the word *mammoth* came from. This thing was huge. It was gigantic. Enormous. Mammoth.

The mammoth jerked his head back and fixed us with one tiny eye. Fortunately, he seemed just

as surprised to see us as we were to see him. Unfortunately, he stood about ten feet taller and weighed about two tons more than us. And most unfortunately, we were standing in his way. We stood face to face, not knowing what to do. Fred bent down slowly and picked up a stick that had broken off to a point. "Our only chance is to scare him off."

"Let's not do anything that might make him mad," I whispered.

"We could turn and run," said Fred. Sam inched backward. "That sounds good to me."

"But we'd probably get trampled from behind."

"That doesn't sound so good to me."

Fred eyed the huge, hairy ancestor of an elephant in front of us. He raised his stick and then threw it as hard as he could. The makeshift spear sailed through the air and stuck the mammoth right between the eyes.

The mammoth blinked and slowly shook its gigantic head and pointy tusks. Fred's spear fell to the ground like a used toothpick. The mammoth lowered those pointy tusks in our direction and trumpeted.

"Time for another disappearing act," I said. "Because now I think you made him mad."

The hairy monster shook its mammoth head again and raised one mammoth foot.

And that's the last thing I saw because we turned and ran for the trees. We dodged around bushes and rocks. The mammoth smashed through the bushes and rocks. We were running as fast as we could, but the mammoth was still gaining on us and there was nowhere to hide.

We ran. Mammoth footsteps shook the ground behind us. We ran. Hot, smelly, mammoth breath blasted the back of my neck. I knew we were goners. But I wondered if our math teacher would believe the note from home: "Dear Mr. Dexter, Please excuse Joe, Sam, and Fred for not doing their math homework. They got run over by a woolly mammoth."

T E N

Fred led the way in an all-out sprint. Sam followed him. I followed Sam. One large, angry woolly mammoth closely followed us all.

We were just about to become woolly mammoth toe jam when Fred yelled, "There." He pointed to two trees about five feet apart. Fred dove between the trees. Sam dove between the trees. I tripped, jumped, hopped, and felt the tip of one giant tusk push me between the trees.

The woolly mammoth's head followed us, but the rest of its monster body didn't. It slammed into the two trees and wedged there fast. The mammoth trumpeted and shook its tusks, but it couldn't move forward or backward. We took one look and ran until we couldn't hear its mad blasts anymore.

We finally collapsed and sat under a giant fern,

just trying to breathe and stop our hearts from pounding.

I searched the prehistoric and unfamiliar forest all around us. "Man," I said. "What next?"

Sam studied the small patch of sky that showed through the branches overhead. "By the look of the overcast sky and setting sun, I would say next we better find shelter before night falls."

"Oh, great," said Fred. "Mr. Brainpower is back with more bright ideas like 'Find shelter before night falls.' I liked you better when you just drooled and said 'Woo woo woo, ma ma ma.'"

"So whose bright idea was it to poke a woolly mammoth with a pointed stick?" said Sam.

"Whose bright idea was it to come to the Stone Age in the first place?" said Fred.

"You almost got us killed."

"You got us lost."

"Nat-Li."

"You're a jerk."

"You're a Neanderthal."

"Wait a minute, you guys," I said. "Who just said 'Nat-Li'?"

We all looked at each other.

"Not me," said Fred.

"Not me," said Sam.

"Nat-Li."

"Over there," said Fred.

We crawled over fallen trees and around smashed rocks, following the sound of the voice calling Nat-Li.

In a few minutes we were standing on the edge of a familiar clearing.

"It's Ma and her clan," I said. "We're back at the cave."

"Yeah," said Fred. "But what happened to the cave?"

Ma and the rest of the women stood next to a huge rock at the base of the cliff. Lin-Say and Jos-Feen pounded on the rock with their fists. Ma called, "Nat-Li."

"The quake must have loosened that boulder and sealed the entrance to the cave," said Sam. "And Nat-Li's trapped inside."

"This is our chance," said Fred. "We push away the stone, save Nat-Li, and become heroes. Then we can ask for anything we want."

"I don't know," I said. "Remember—"

But I was too late. Fred was already in the

middle of the clearing calling, "Time Warp Trio to the rescue." We didn't have much choice but to follow him.

Fred didn't even give anyone a chance to be surprised. He walked right up to the rock and started calling out instructions. "Lin-Say, Jos-Feen, Sam, and Joe on this side. Push on three. One, two, *three*."

We pushed. The stone rocked about an inch and fell back.

"More muscle," called Fred. He waved the other women over to push. "One, two, *three*."

The stone rolled about two inches, then fell back.

"We'll never be able to move this," I panted. "It must weigh a ton."

"Ma," a voice called faintly from behind the stone.

"We just need more muscle," said Fred. "Duh! That's it. They can't be too far away." Fred cupped his hands and yelled into the forest. *"Duh, Duh! Boog, boog!"*

Ma, Lin-Say, and Jos-Feen looked at Fred like he had lost his mind.

"Duh, Duh! Boog, boog!" yelled Fred.

And you won't believe it, because Sam and I didn't either, but like magic, Duh and his whole band of guys appeared out of the trees.

Fred dragged Duh out into the open and over to the rock. The whole time he kept making pushing motions and talking about boog. The rest of the guys followed cautiously. And in less time than it takes to say "Operation Rescue," Fred had Ma, Duh, men, women, Lin-Say, Jos-Feen, Sam, and me on one side of the boulder.

"All together now," yelled Fred. "One, two, *three*."

Everyone pushed.

The stone rolled slowly up . . . up . . . up . . . and then fell back with a thud.

Everyone collapsed to the ground. Shadows grew longer as the sun sank lower.

"It's no good," said Sam. "We can't all push in that small of a space."

"Ma?" Nat-Li called through the rock.

"But she'll die in there," said Fred.

I looked at Ma. I looked at Duh. I knew they didn't speak our language. But the look on their faces said the same thing.

ELEVEN

Wait a minute," said Sam. "Let's figure this out." Sam started pacing back and forth and talking to himself. "Nat-Li is trapped behind the rock. If 5 people can move the rock 1 inch, how many people will it take to move the rock 24 inches?" Sam grabbed a stick and scribbled in the sand. "5 people for every inch times 24 inches equals . . . 120 people."

"So let's do it," said Fred.

"There are only two small problems," said Sam. "One: we don't have 120 people. And two: even if we did, we couldn't fit 120 people on one side of the rock. We need a more simple solution."

The word *simple* rang a bell in my head.

"What about your pal, Archimedes?" I said.

"He won't be around for another 39,000 years or so," said Sam.

"No, I mean what about that lever thing?"

"Joe, you're a genius," yelled Sam. "Give us a fulcrum, a long enough lever, and a place to stand, and the Time Warp Trio will move the world . . . or at least one very large rock."

Fred grabbed a sturdy-looking branch.

I rolled a small stone near one side of the boulder.

Our Stone Age audience watched us closely. We jammed the stick under the boulder and over the smaller rock. The three of us pulled down on our lever. The boulder rocked and then slowly rolled up. The stick creaked, bent, and snapped. We landed in a heap, holding half a lever.

Duh looked carefully at the broken stick. He walked off into the woods and came back carrying a log ten feet long and twice as thick as our original lever.

"Now you're thinking," said Sam.

Duh wedged the lever under the boulder just like he'd seen us do. He pulled down. The boulder rocked.

We grabbed the lever and pulled down. The
boulder rolled up. Lin-Say, Jos-feen, and Ma
pulled the lever down. The boulder rose up, tee-
tered, and suddenly rolled off to one side, crash-
ing down the hill.

Nat-Li raced out of the cave and danced
around hugging everyone in sight—Ma, Lin-Say,
Jos-Feen, Fred, Sam, me, and even Duh. I
couldn't tell for sure through the wild beard, but
I think Duh's face turned an embarrassed red.

Ma made hand motions and gave orders to her clan. All the women nodded and smiled. Duh and his men nodded and smiled. We had absolutely no idea what was going on, but we nodded and smiled.

That night we had the greatest party ever thrown in the Stone Age. The women showed Duh's men how to build huge roaring bonfires. Ma's clan brought out a feast of fruit, nuts, flat bread, stews, and a dark fizzy drink.

"Caveman Cola," said Fred. He took one of the fresher-looking pieces of meat from one of the men and held it over the fire on a stick.

"Boog?" asked Duh.

"No. Cooked boog," answered Fred. "Burger."

"Booger?"

"Burger."

Fred folded a piece of the bread around the cooked meat and handed it to Duh.

Duh took a bite and smiled. *"Burger."*

Sam finished fitting the last of four circular

68

pieces of wood onto the ends of two sticks he had tied to a small log. Lin-Say and Jos-Feen watched closely. "Wheels," said Sam. "These are wheels. We need these on our skateboards so we can do three-sixties."

"Three-sixties?" said Lin-Say.

"That's right," said Sam. "That stands for the three hundred and sixty degrees in a circle, but I think we'll have to invent numbers and circles before I explain all that. For now we'll just stick with skateboards."

"Three-sixties," said Jos-Feen.

I found my straw and played a kazoo kind of version of "Three Blind Mice." "Music," I said. Nat-Li clapped, and then honked her own tune on the straw.

Someone started drumming. People started dancing around the fire. Then Duh acted out the rescue.

Nat-Li played herself, crouching off on one side of the fire, looking afraid.

Three guys played the rock. Ma tried to push them. Fred and Ma tried to push them. We all tried to push them. They wouldn't budge.

The drums beat faster. Sam and Duh pretended

to wedge a stick under the rock guys. Duh and Sam jumped. The drums stopped. The three guys rolled off into the darkness and Nat-Li jumped triumphantly into the firelight.

The drums started up again. Everyone laughed and danced, and then we did the whole thing over again. And again. And again. And again. And again until the bonfires dimmed low and the full moon began to sink in the lightening sky.

"Hamburgers, music, and parties—not a bad start on civilization," said Fred.

Sam doodled *A, B, C,* and *1, 2, 3* in the sand. "There might be some hope for the species after all. Tomorrow we'll start numbers and letters. Who knows. By 39,999 b.c. we may be able to put together a book."

"I still can't believe there were no paintings in the cave," I said.

"They took us everywhere and we saw everything," said Fred. "It must be in some other cave."

Sam traced three stick figures.

Nat-Li looked at Sam's scribbles and then suddenly jumped up and ran off.

"Was it something I said?" asked Sam.

"No," said Fred. "I think it's your . . . problem dandruff." Fred laughed and punched Sam in the arm.

Nat-Li came back dragging Ma by the arm. Ma took one look, said something to her clan, and we were instantly surrounded by women half-leading, half-pushing us into the cave.

"I didn't mean it," said Sam.

"I didn't do it," said Fred.

Someone lit torches. We were swept through the main cave and back to the entrance of the small cave with the bars.

"Not again," said Fred.

Ma took a torch and motioned for us to follow. We looked at the prehistoric crowd in the weird torchlight behind us. Duh held up one hand. Nat-Li waved her straw. "Three-sixties," said Jos-Feen. Lin-Say cupped her hands to her mouth like a megaphone and called, "Joe Sam Fred, o-kay o-kay."

"It doesn't look like we have much choice," I said.

And we followed Ma into the dark cave.

TWELVE

The little cave turned out to be much bigger than we thought. A narrow passageway, only big enough for one person at a time, spiraled back, deep into the earth. The noise of the main cave fell away, and we followed Ma in spooky silence. The passage spiraled tighter and tighter until we were at last forced to crawl on our hands and knees. We followed the flickering torch and listened to the sound of our own breathing. We squeezed through one last crack in the rock, and suddenly found ourselves standing in an immense underground room.

Weird, drippy-looking columns of stone rose on all sides from floor to ceiling. Crystals sparkled in the torchlight. We stood gawking in amazement until Ma motioned us over to a large flat wall of rock.

She pointed to the wall and said, "Joe Sam Fred."

We looked and saw a spiral of painted stars, moons, handprints, and three stick figures on the cave wall.

"It's the painting," said Fred.

"It must be the very first version of *The Book*," I said.

"It's a miracle," said Sam.

Ma put Fred's Cubs hat gently on his head. She touched each of us on the head. And I could have sworn she said, "Eena. Meena. Mina." Then she stepped back and with a wave of her torch said, "Mo."

The flame flickered. A familiar green mist started to swirl around the cave. Ma raised both arms and laughed. And before we could say a word of thanks or good-bye, we were swallowed up and gone.

THIRTEEN

Sam sneezed. The green mist melted away. And Fred, Sam, and I were standing back in my room, loaded with equipment and fully clothed as if we had never been anywhere.

Fred shook his head and pulled on his Cubs hat.

I felt something in my hands and looked down to see I was holding *The Book.*

Sam cleaned his glasses, then looked at my clock and calendar. "Four-thirty. 1992."

And at that very moment my mom called, "Joseph Arthur?" and opened the door.

We were caught red-handed.

I was still trying to think of a good excuse to explain why we had emptied the kitchen drawers and closets when my mom looked us over and said, "Traveling?"

"We . . . we . . . we . . ."

My mom looked at *The Book* in my hands and shook her head. "I don't know what your uncle was thinking when he gave you that present."

"Well you see, Mom, we were just getting ready to go . . . uh, camping," I said.

"Yeah, that's it," said Fred. "We were going camping."

Sam looked around the room and pretended to clean his glasses again.

My mom looked the three of us over once more and shook her head. "But I suppose he was about your age when I first showed him *The Book*."

I was still trying to think up a better excuse when that last line sunk in.

"You showed who? What?"

My mom raised one eyebrow and laughed, looking a lot like a certain woman we had just left 41,992 years and a minute ago. "Well, who do you think taught her little brother Joe the magic he knows?"

POP QUIZ

1. If Mr. Sleeby walks an average speed of 2.5 miles per hour, how many miles does he walk in 4 hours?

(a) *10.*

(b) *12.*

(c) *I don't know how far Mr. Sleeby walks in 4 hours.*

(d) *I don't care how far Mr. Sleeby walks in 4 hours.*

(e) *I can't tell you how far Mr. Sleeby walks in 4 hours because I've just been run over by a woolly mammoth.*

2. Given a fulcrum, a long enough lever, and a place to stand, a person could theoretically move

(a) *The world.*

(b) *To Alaska.*

(c) *I don't know.*

(d) *I don't care.*

(e) *I can't tell you because I've just been run over by a woolly mammoth.*

3. Archimedes was

(a) *A Greek mathematician.*

(b) *A shortstop for the Chicago Cubs.*

(c) *I don't know.*

(d) *I don't care.*

(e) *I can't tell you because I've just been run over by a woolly mammoth.*

4. Fred, Sam, and Joe start in the year A.D. 1992 and travel back in time to the year 40,000 B.C. They are trapped in a cave by 4 wooden bars. If it takes each guy 20 minutes to saw through half a bar, do you think they'll escape in time?

(a) Yes.

(b) No.

(c) Maybe.

(d) None of the above.

(e) I can't tell you because I've just been run over
   by a woolly mammoth.

5. This book costs $10.99. Dinosaurs became extinct 65 million years ago. Cro-Magnon man, our direct ancestor, lived about 40,000 years ago. If you were a woolly mammoth, *then* would you do your math homework?

(a) 64,040,011.

(b) $2.95.

(c) What?

(d) Leave me alone.

(e) I can't tell you because woolly mammoths can't talk.

SCORE YOURSELF!

For every *a* answer, give yourself 5 points.
For every *b* answer, give yourself 4 points.
For every *c* answer, give yourself 3 points.
For every *d* answer, give yourself 2 points.
For every *e* answer, give yourself 1 point.

GRADES

25–21 Son of Archimedes
20–16 Distant Cousin of Archimedes
15–11 Didn't Know Archimedes
10– 6 Doesn't Care About Archimedes
 5– 0 Should Really See a Doctor About That Mammoth Problem